D1622781

NA NIM

MARVEL® SUPER HERO SQUAD

WHEN SLURKS THE SLIME!

WRITER: Todd Dezago
ARTISTS: Leonel Castellani & Marcelo DiChiara
COLORS: Sotocolor
LETTERS: Dave Sharpe

SUPER HERO SQUAD STRIPS
WRITER: Paul Tobin
ARTISTS: Marcelo DiChiara, Todd Nauck & Dario Brizuela
COLORS: Chris Sotomayor
LETTERS: Blambot's Nate Piekos

ASSISTANT EDITOR: Michael Horwitz
EDITOR: Nathan Cosby

Spotlight

Visit us at www.abdopublishing.com

Reinforced library bound edition published in 2011 by Spotlight, a division of the ABDO Group, 8000 West 78th Street, Edina, Minnesota 55439. Spotlight produces high-quality reinforced library bound editions for schools and libraries. Published by agreement with Marvel Characters, Inc.

Printed in the United States of America, North Mankato, Minnesota.
102010
012011
♻ This book contains at least 10% recycled materials.

Library of Congress Cataloging-in-Publication Data

Dezago, Todd.
  When slurks the slime! / Todd Dezago, writer ; Leonel Castellani & Marcelo DiChiara, artists ; Sotocolor, colors ; Dave Sharpe, letters. -- Reinforced library bound ed.
     p. cm. -- (Super hero squad)
  "Marvel."
  ISBN 978-1-59961-863-0
  1. Graphic novels. [1. Graphic novels. 2. Superheroes--Fiction.] I. Castellani, Leonel, ill. II. Dichiara, Marcelo, ill. III. Title.
  PZ7.7.D508Wh 2011
  741.5'973--dc22

                                        2010027327

All Spotlight books have reinforced library bindings and
are manufactured in the United States of America.

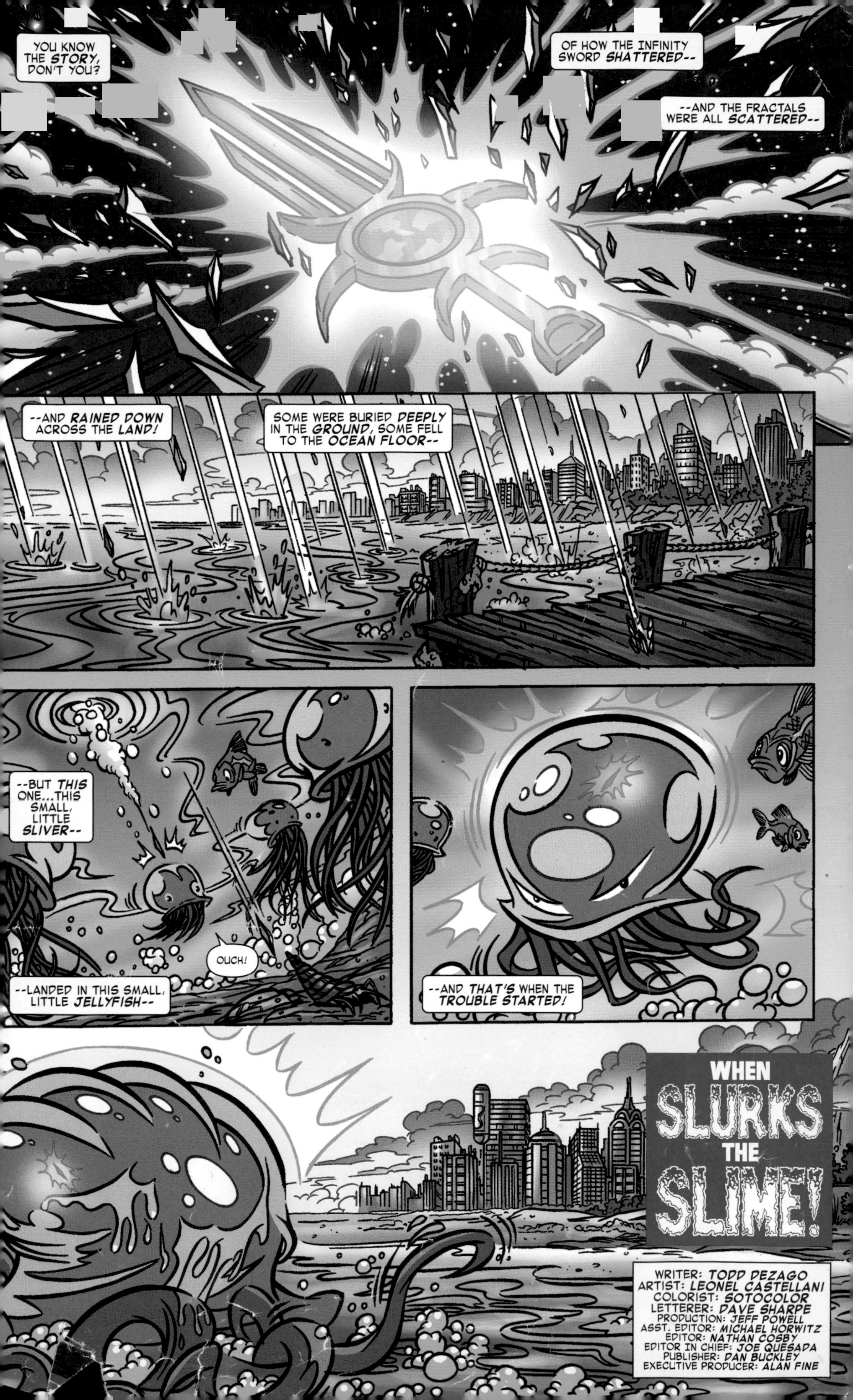

YOU KNOW THE STORY, DON'T YOU?
OF HOW THE INFINITY SWORD SHATTERED--
--AND THE FRACTALS WERE ALL SCATTERED--
--AND RAINED DOWN ACROSS THE LAND!
SOME WERE BURIED DEEPLY IN THE GROUND, SOME FELL TO THE OCEAN FLOOR--
--BUT THIS ONE...THIS SMALL, LITTLE SLIVER--
OUCH!
--LANDED IN THIS SMALL, LITTLE JELLYFISH--
--AND THAT'S WHEN THE TROUBLE STARTED!
WHEN SLURKS THE SLIME!
WRITER: TODD DEZAGO
ARTIST: LEONEL CASTELLANI
COLORIST: SOTOCOLOR
LETTERER: DAVE SHARPE
PRODUCTION: JEFF POWELL
ASST. EDITOR: MICHAEL HORWITZ
EDITOR: NATHAN COSBY
EDITOR IN CHIEF: JOE QUESADA
PUBLISHER: DAN BUCKLEY
EXECUTIVE PRODUCER: ALAN FINE

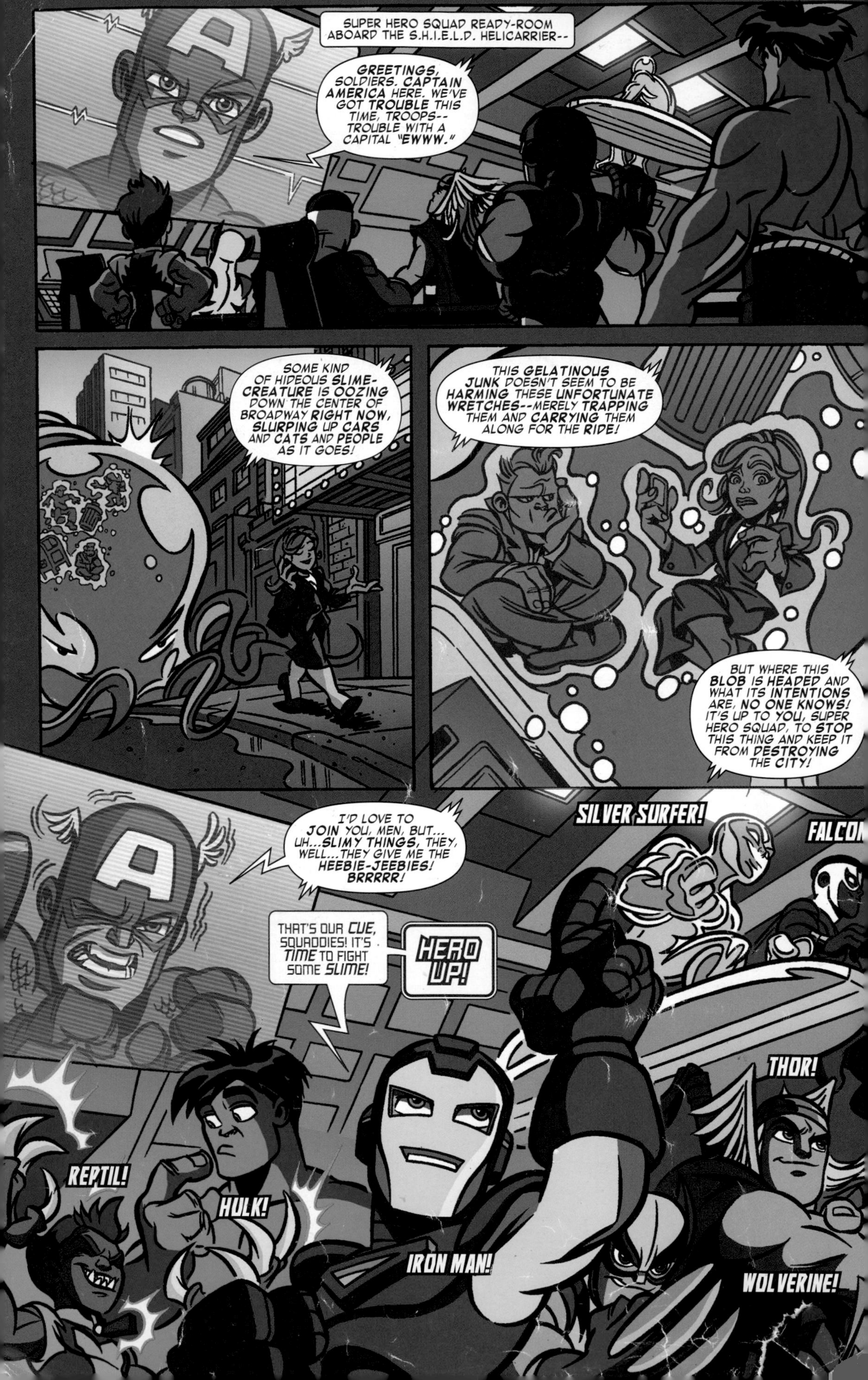
SUPER HERO SQUAD READY-ROOM ABOARD THE S.H.I.E.L.D. HELICARRIER--
GREETINGS, SOLDIERS. CAPTAIN AMERICA HERE. WE'VE GOT TROUBLE THIS TIME, TROOPS--TROUBLE WITH A CAPITAL "EWWW."
SOME KIND OF HIDEOUS SLIME-CREATURE IS OOZING DOWN THE CENTER OF BROADWAY RIGHT NOW, SLURPING UP CARS AND CATS AND PEOPLE AS IT GOES!
THIS GELATINOUS JUNK DOESN'T SEEM TO BE HARMING THESE UNFORTUNATE WRETCHES--MERELY TRAPPING THEM AND CARRYING THEM ALONG FOR THE RIDE!
BUT WHERE THIS BLOB IS HEADED AND WHAT ITS INTENTIONS ARE, NO ONE KNOWS! IT'S UP TO YOU, SUPER HERO SQUAD, TO STOP THIS THING AND KEEP IT FROM DESTROYING THE CITY!
I'D LOVE TO JOIN YOU, MEN, BUT... UH...SLIMY THINGS, THEY, WELL...THEY GIVE ME THE HEEBIE-JEEBIES! BRRRRR!
SILVER SURFER!
FALCON
THAT'S OUR CUE, SQUADDIES! IT'S TIME TO FIGHT SOME SLIME!
HERO UP!
THOR!
REPTIL!
HULK!
IRON MAN!
WOLVERINE!

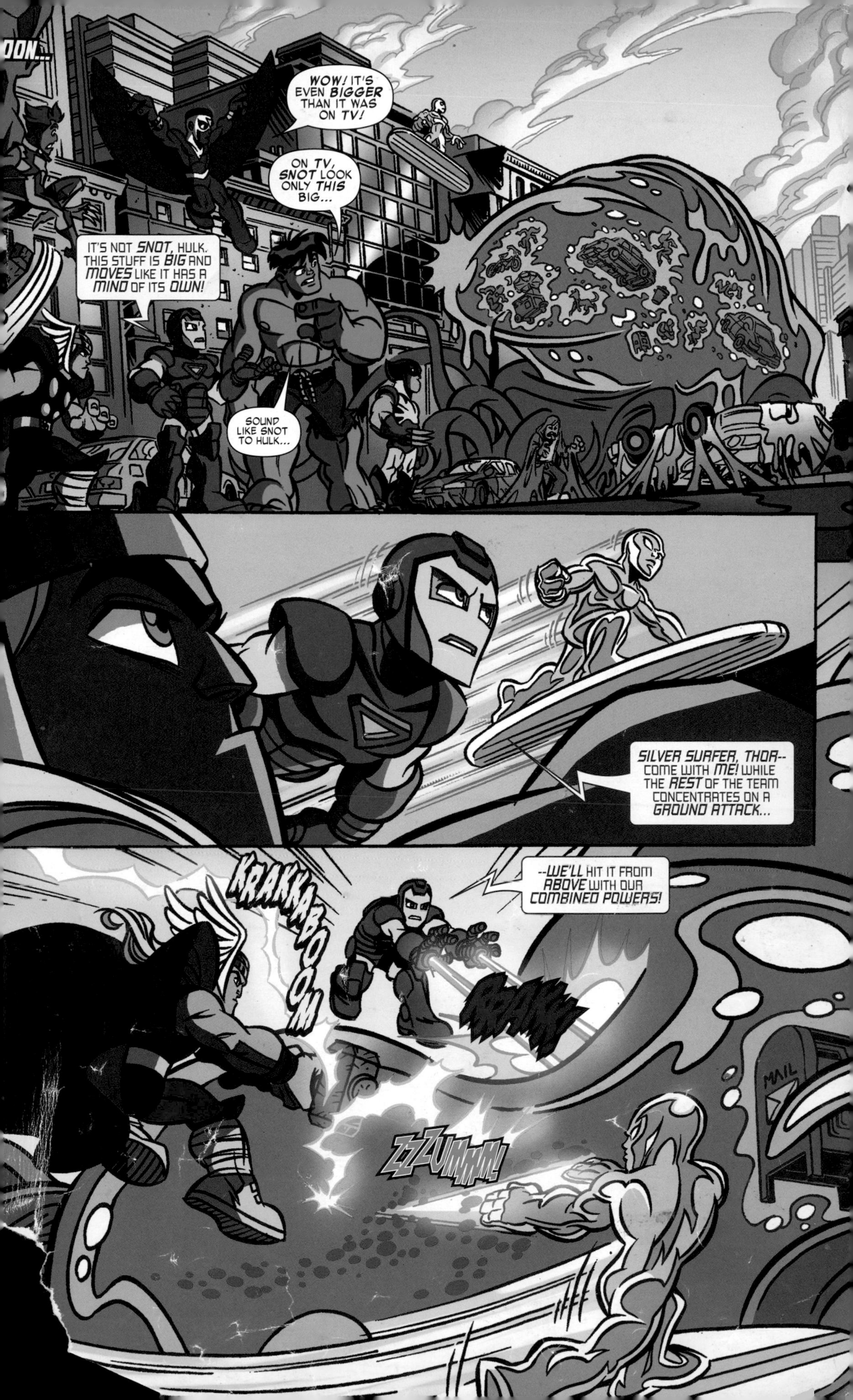

WOW! IT'S EVEN BIGGER THAN IT WAS ON TV!
ON TV, SNOT LOOK ONLY THIS BIG...
IT'S NOT SNOT, HULK. THIS STUFF IS BIG AND MOVES LIKE IT HAS A MIND OF ITS OWN!
SOUND LIKE SNOT TO HULK...
SILVER SURFER, THOR-- COME WITH ME! WHILE THE REST OF THE TEAM CONCENTRATES ON A GROUND ATTACK...
--WE'LL HIT IT FROM ABOVE WITH OUR COMBINED POWERS!
KRAKKABOOOM
ZZZUMMM!
MAIL

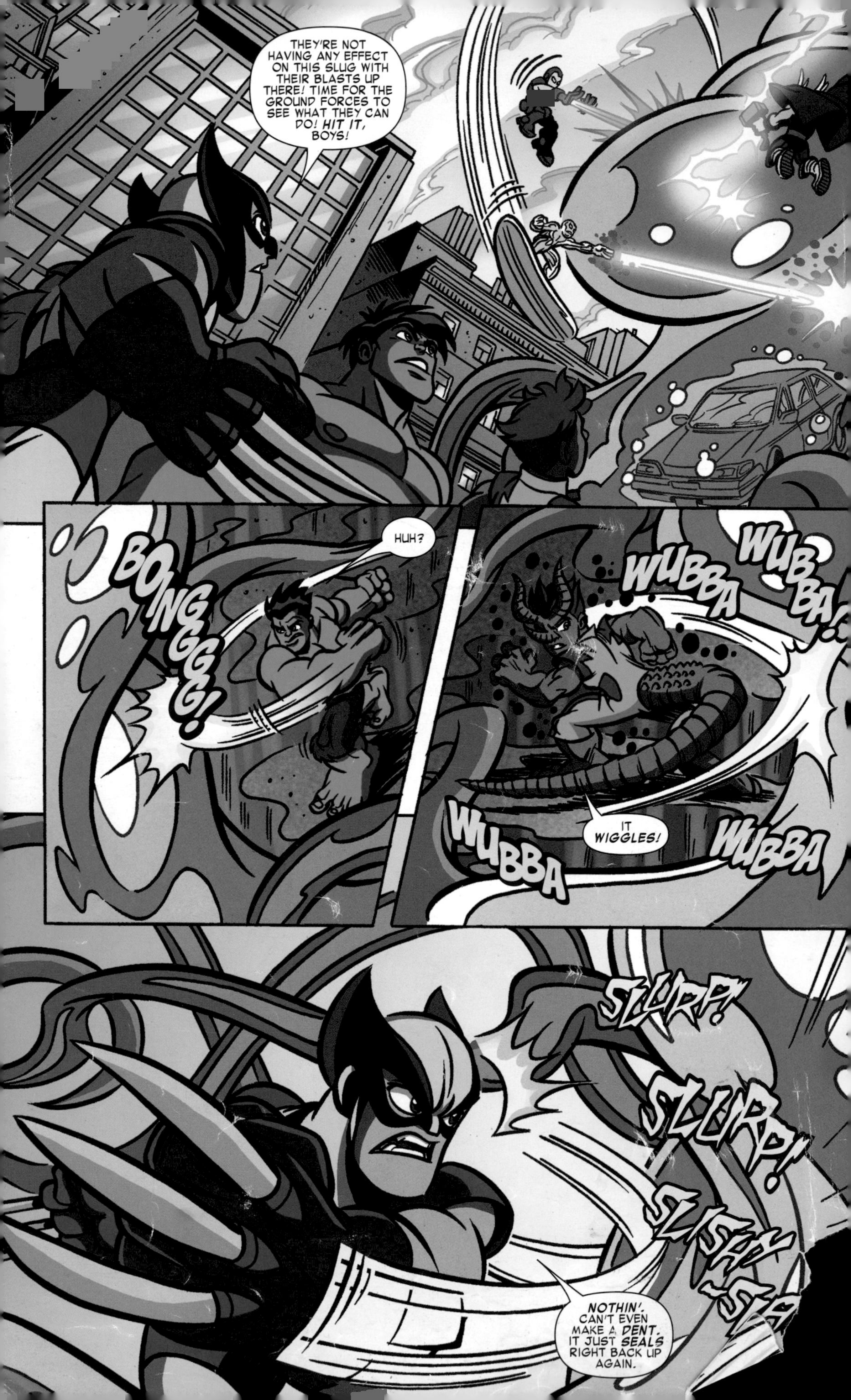

THEY'RE NOT HAVING ANY EFFECT ON THIS SLUG WITH THEIR BLASTS UP THERE! TIME FOR THE GROUND FORCES TO SEE WHAT THEY CAN DO! *HIT IT,* BOYS!
BOINGGG!
HUH?
WUBBA
WUBBA!
IT *WIGGLES!*
WUBBA
WUBBA
SLURP!
SLURP!
NOTHIN'. CAN'T EVEN MAKE A *DENT.* IT JUST *SEALS* RIGHT BACK UP AGAIN.

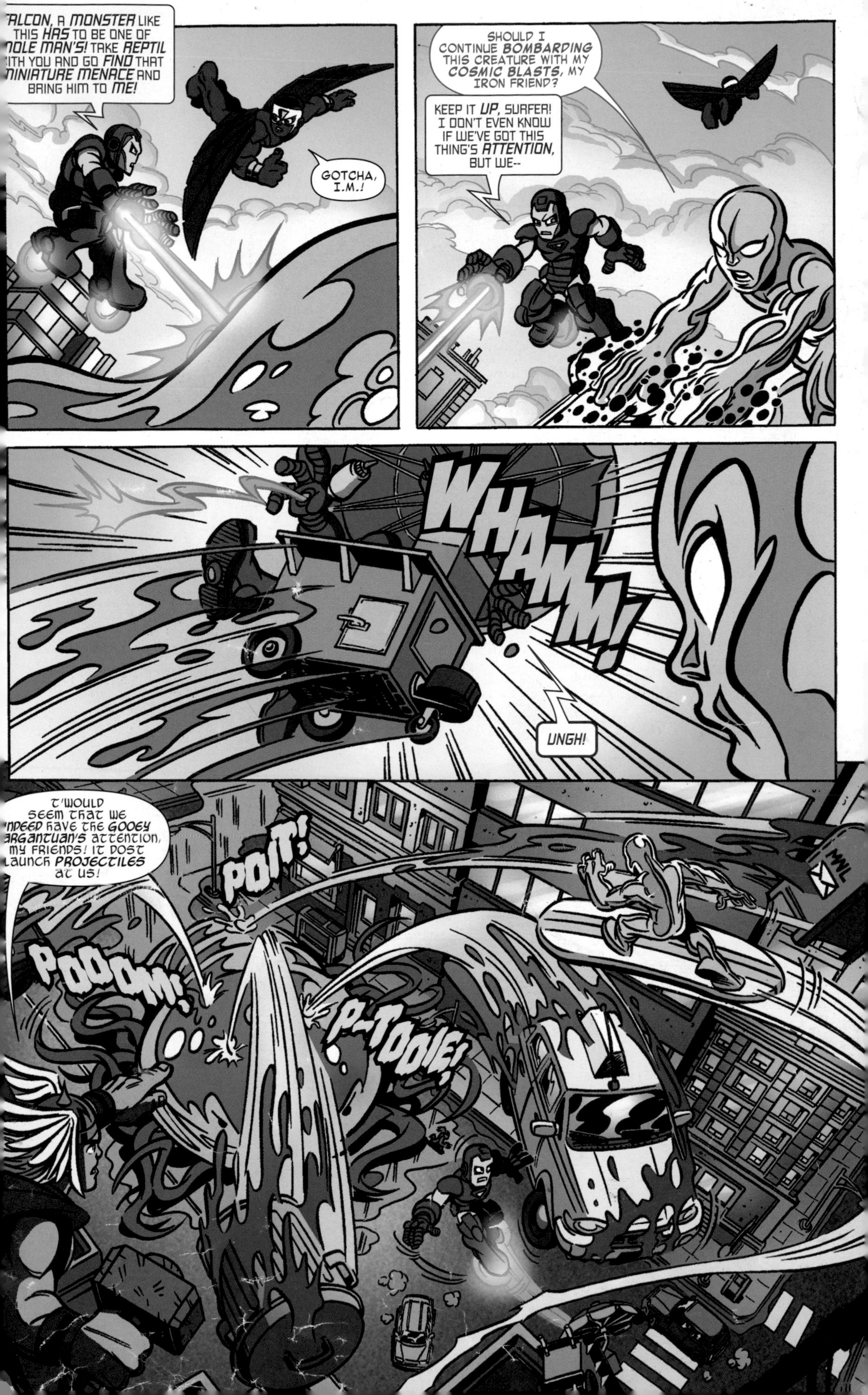

ALCON, A MONSTER LIKE THIS HAS TO BE ONE OF OLE MAN'S! TAKE REPTIL ITH YOU AND GO FIND THAT INIATURE MENACE AND BRING HIM TO ME!
GOTCHA, I.M.!
SHOULD I CONTINUE BOMBARDING THIS CREATURE WITH MY COSMIC BLASTS, MY IRON FRIEND?
KEEP IT UP, SURFER! I DON'T EVEN KNOW IF WE'VE GOT THIS THING'S ATTENTION, BUT WE--
WHAMMM!
UNGH!
T'WOULD SEEM THAT WE NDEED HAVE THE GOOEY ARGANTUAN'S ATTENTION, MY FRIENDS! IT DOST LAUNCH PROJECTILES AT US!
POIT!
POOOM!
P-TOOIE!
MAIL

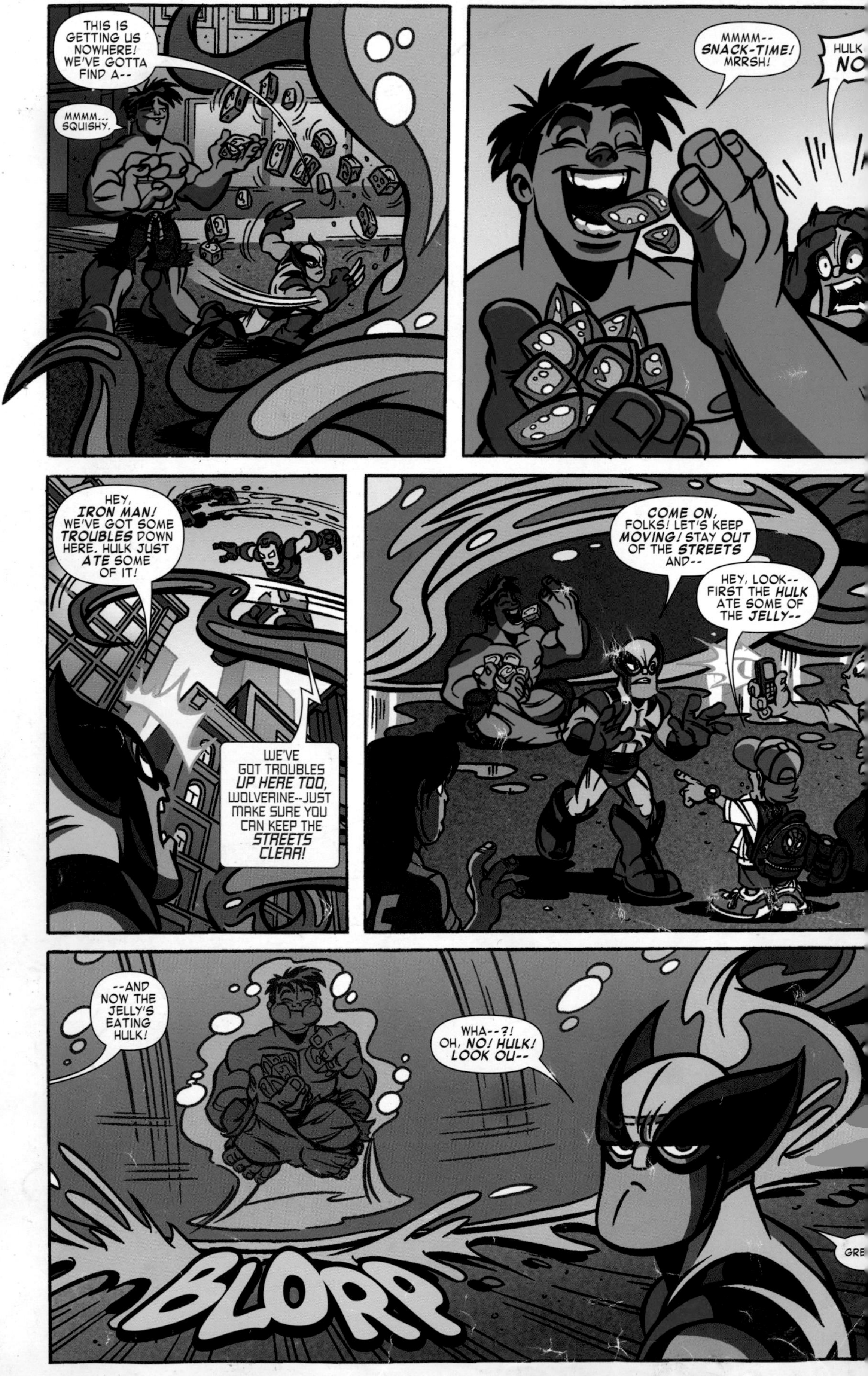
THIS IS GETTING US NOWHERE! WE'VE GOTTA FIND A--
MMMM... SQUISHY.
MMMM-- SNACK-TIME! MRRSH!
HULK
HEY, IRON MAN! WE'VE GOT SOME TROUBLES DOWN HERE. HULK JUST ATE SOME OF IT!
WE'VE GOT TROUBLES UP HERE TOO, WOLVERINE--JUST MAKE SURE YOU CAN KEEP THE STREETS CLEAR!
COME ON, FOLKS! LET'S KEEP MOVING! STAY OUT OF THE STREETS AND--
HEY, LOOK-- FIRST THE HULK ATE SOME OF THE JELLY--
--AND NOW THE JELLY'S EATING HULK!
WHA--?! OH, NO! HULK! LOOK OU--
BLOPP

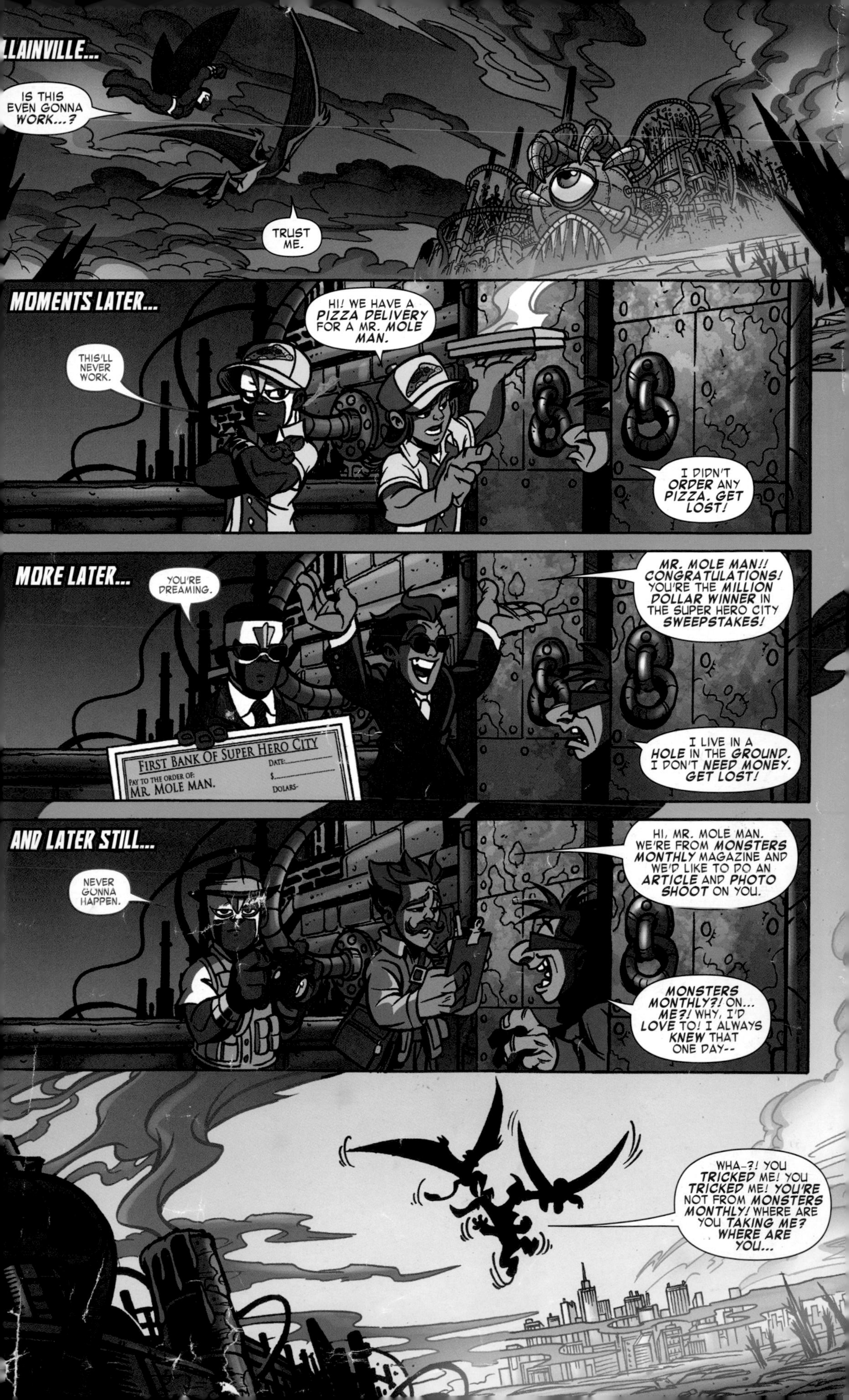
LLAINVILLE...
IS THIS EVEN GONNA WORK...?
TRUST ME.
MOMENTS LATER...
THIS'LL NEVER WORK.
HI! WE HAVE A PIZZA DELIVERY FOR A MR. MOLE MAN.
I DIDN'T ORDER ANY PIZZA. GET LOST!
MORE LATER...
YOU'RE DREAMING.
MR. MOLE MAN!! CONGRATULATIONS! YOU'RE THE MILLION DOLLAR WINNER IN THE SUPER HERO CITY SWEEPSTAKES!
FIRST BANK OF SUPER HERO CITY
DATE:
PAY TO THE ORDER OF:
MR. MOLE MAN.
$
DOLARS-
I LIVE IN A HOLE IN THE GROUND. I DON'T NEED MONEY. GET LOST!
AND LATER STILL...
NEVER GONNA HAPPEN.
HI, MR. MOLE MAN. WE'RE FROM MONSTERS MONTHLY MAGAZINE AND WE'D LIKE TO DO AN ARTICLE AND PHOTO SHOOT ON YOU.
MONSTERS MONTHLY?! ON... ME?! WHY, I'D LOVE TO! I ALWAYS KNEW THAT ONE DAY--
WHA-?! YOU TRICKED ME! YOU TRICKED ME! YOU'RE NOT FROM MONSTERS MONTHLY! WHERE ARE YOU TAKING ME? WHERE ARE YOU...

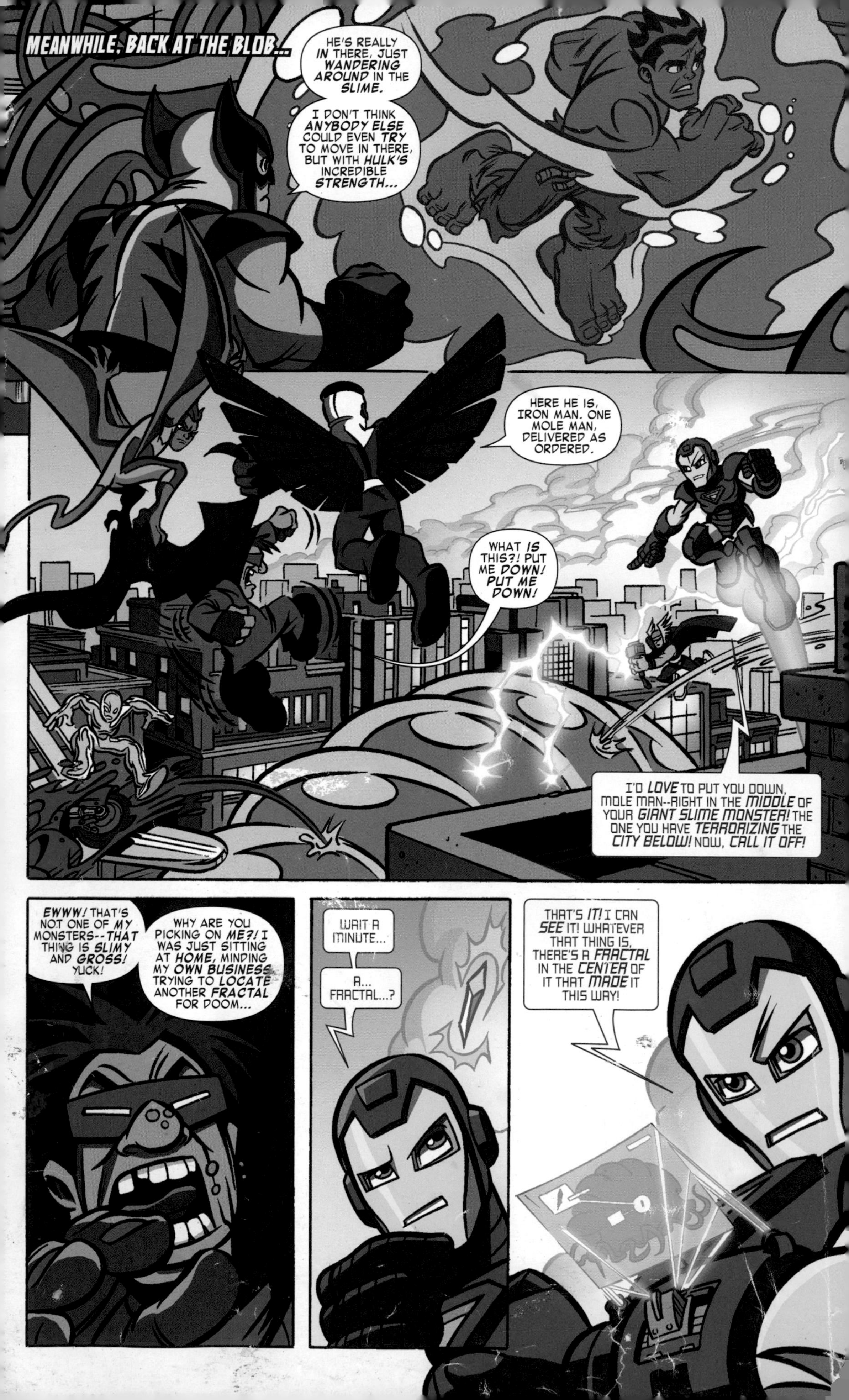
MEANWHILE, BACK AT THE BLOB...
HE'S REALLY IN THERE, JUST WANDERING AROUND IN THE SLIME.
I DON'T THINK ANYBODY ELSE COULD EVEN TRY TO MOVE IN THERE, BUT WITH HULK'S INCREDIBLE STRENGTH...
HERE HE IS, IRON MAN. ONE MOLE MAN, DELIVERED AS ORDERED.
WHAT IS THIS?! PUT ME DOWN! PUT ME DOWN!
I'D LOVE TO PUT YOU DOWN, MOLE MAN--RIGHT IN THE MIDDLE OF YOUR GIANT SLIME MONSTER! THE ONE YOU HAVE TERRORIZING THE CITY BELOW! NOW, CALL IT OFF!
EWWW! THAT'S NOT ONE OF MY MONSTERS--THAT THING IS SLIMY AND GROSS! YUCK!
WHY ARE YOU PICKING ON ME?! I WAS JUST SITTING AT HOME, MINDING MY OWN BUSINESS TRYING TO LOCATE ANOTHER FRACTAL FOR DOOM...
WAIT A MINUTE...
A... FRACTAL...?
THAT'S IT! I CAN SEE IT! WHATEVER THAT THING IS, THERE'S A FRACTAL IN THE CENTER OF IT THAT MADE IT THIS WAY!

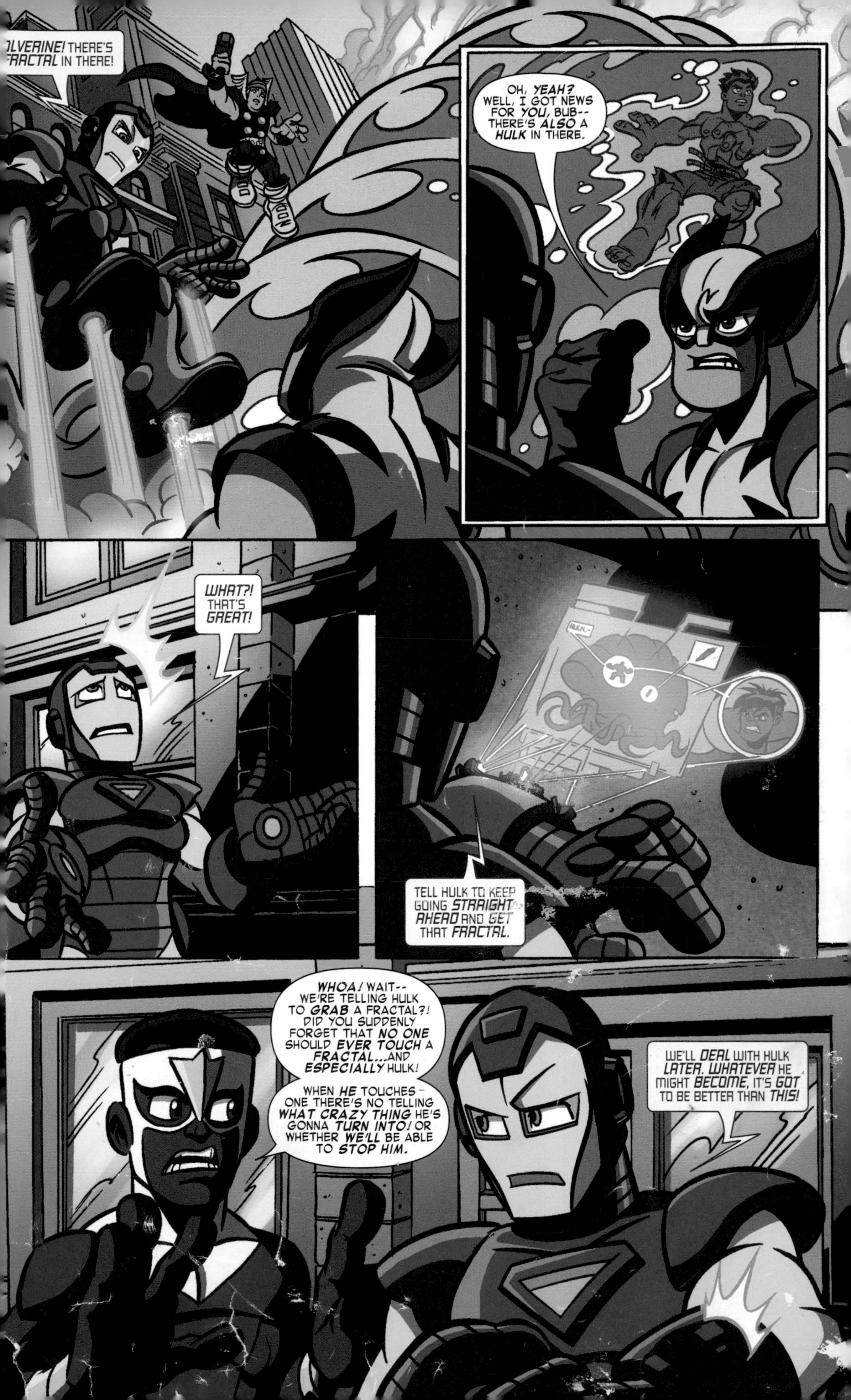

LVERINE! THERE'S FRACTAL IN THERE!
OH, YEAH? WELL, I GOT NEWS FOR YOU, BUB-- THERE'S ALSO A HULK IN THERE.
WHAT?! THAT'S GREAT!
HULK--
TELL HULK TO KEEP GOING STRAIGHT AHEAD AND GET THAT FRACTAL.
WHOA! WAIT-- WE'RE TELLING HULK TO GRAB A FRACTAL?! DID YOU SUDDENLY FORGET THAT NO ONE SHOULD EVER TOUCH A FRACTAL...AND ESPECIALLY HULK!
WHEN HE TOUCHES ONE THERE'S NO TELLING WHAT CRAZY THING HE'S GONNA TURN INTO! OR WHETHER WE'LL BE ABLE TO STOP HIM.
WE'LL DEAL WITH HULK LATER. WHATEVER HE MIGHT BECOME, IT'S GOT TO BE BETTER THAN THIS!

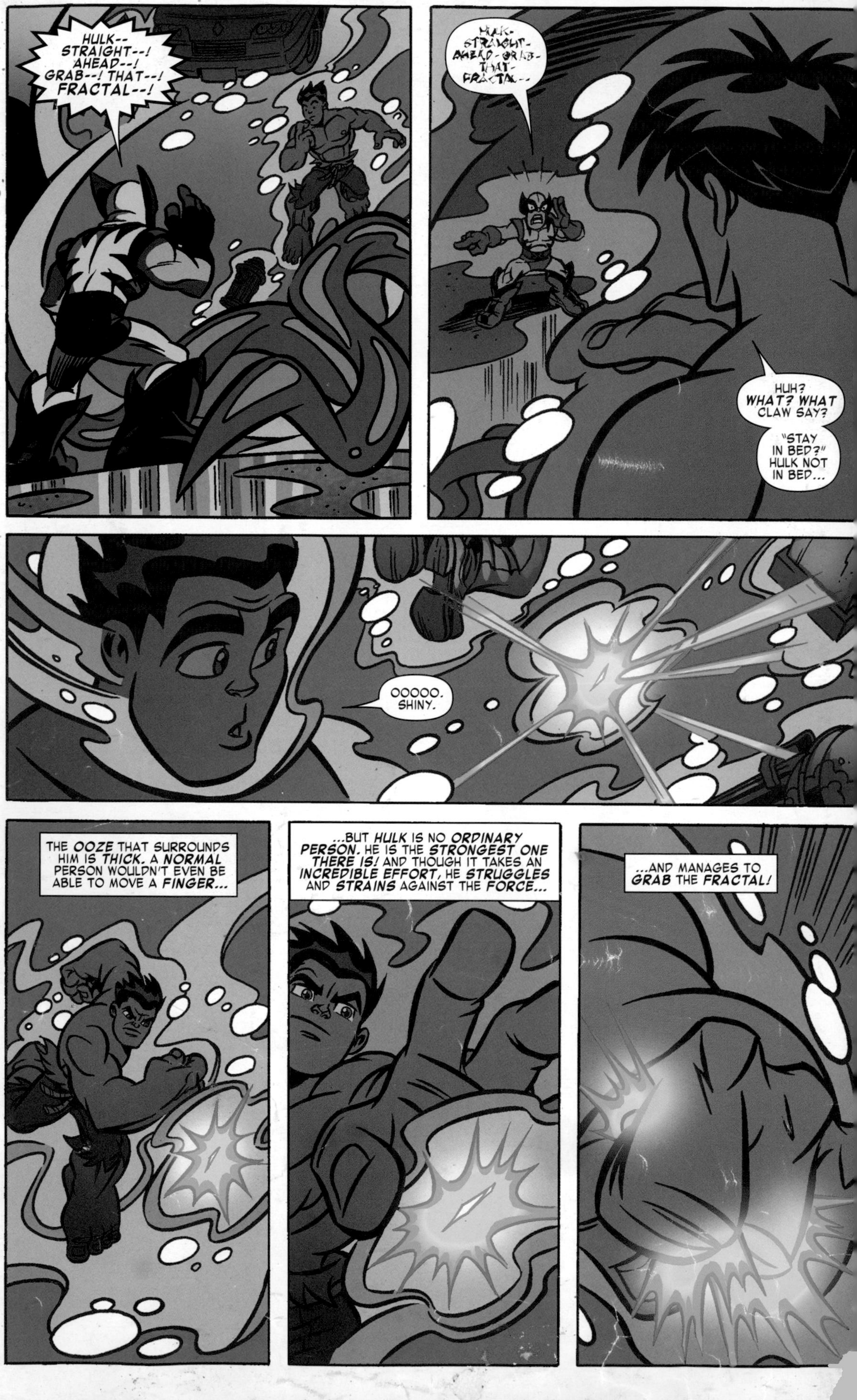
HULK-- STRAIGHT--! AHEAD--! GRAB--! THAT--! FRACTAL--!
HULK- STRAIGHT- AHEAD- GRAB- THAT- FRACTAL--
HUH? WHAT? WHAT CLAW SAY?
"STAY IN BED?" HULK NOT IN BED...
OOOOO. SHINY.
THE OOZE THAT SURROUNDS HIM IS THICK. A NORMAL PERSON WOULDN'T EVEN BE ABLE TO MOVE A FINGER...
...BUT HULK IS NO ORDINARY PERSON. HE IS THE STRONGEST ONE THERE IS! AND THOUGH IT TAKES AN INCREDIBLE EFFORT, HE STRUGGLES AND STRAINS AGAINST THE FORCE...
...AND MANAGES TO GRAB THE FRACTAL!

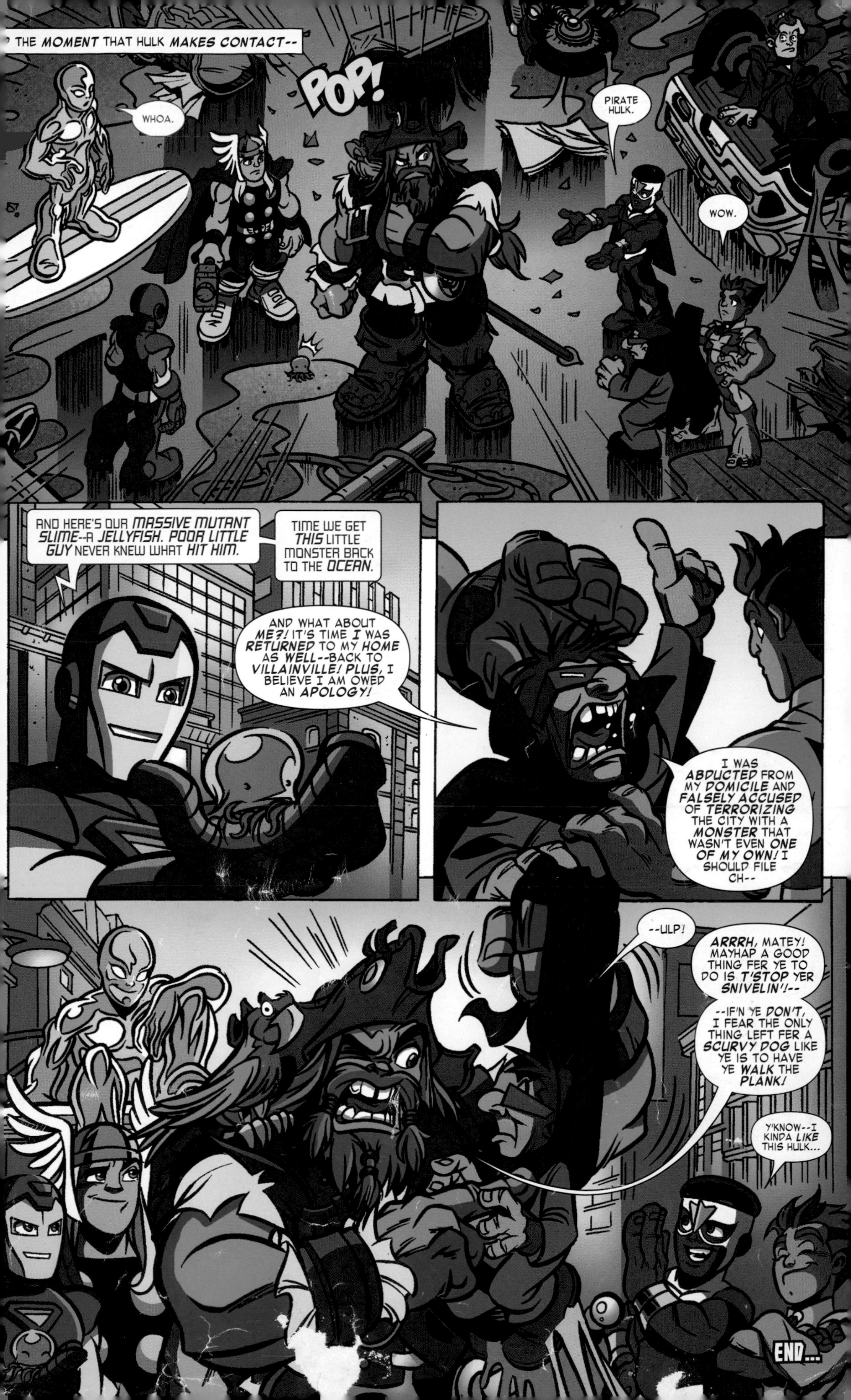
THE MOMENT THAT HULK MAKES CONTACT--
POP!
WHOA.
PIRATE HULK.
WOW.
AND HERE'S OUR MASSIVE MUTANT SLIME--A JELLYFISH. POOR LITTLE GUY NEVER KNEW WHAT HIT HIM.
TIME WE GET THIS LITTLE MONSTER BACK TO THE OCEAN.
AND WHAT ABOUT ME?! IT'S TIME I WAS RETURNED TO MY HOME AS WELL--BACK TO VILLAINVILLE! PLUS, I BELIEVE I AM OWED AN APOLOGY!
I WAS ABDUCTED FROM MY DOMICILE AND FALSELY ACCUSED OF TERRORIZING THE CITY WITH A MONSTER THAT WASN'T EVEN ONE OF MY OWN! I SHOULD FILE CH--
--ULP!
ARRRH, MATEY! MAYHAP A GOOD THING FER YE TO DO IS T'STOP YER SNIVELIN'!--
--IF'N YE DON'T, I FEAR THE ONLY THING LEFT FER A SCURVY DOG LIKE YE IS TO HAVE YE WALK THE PLANK!
Y'KNOW--I KINDA LIKE THIS HULK...
END...

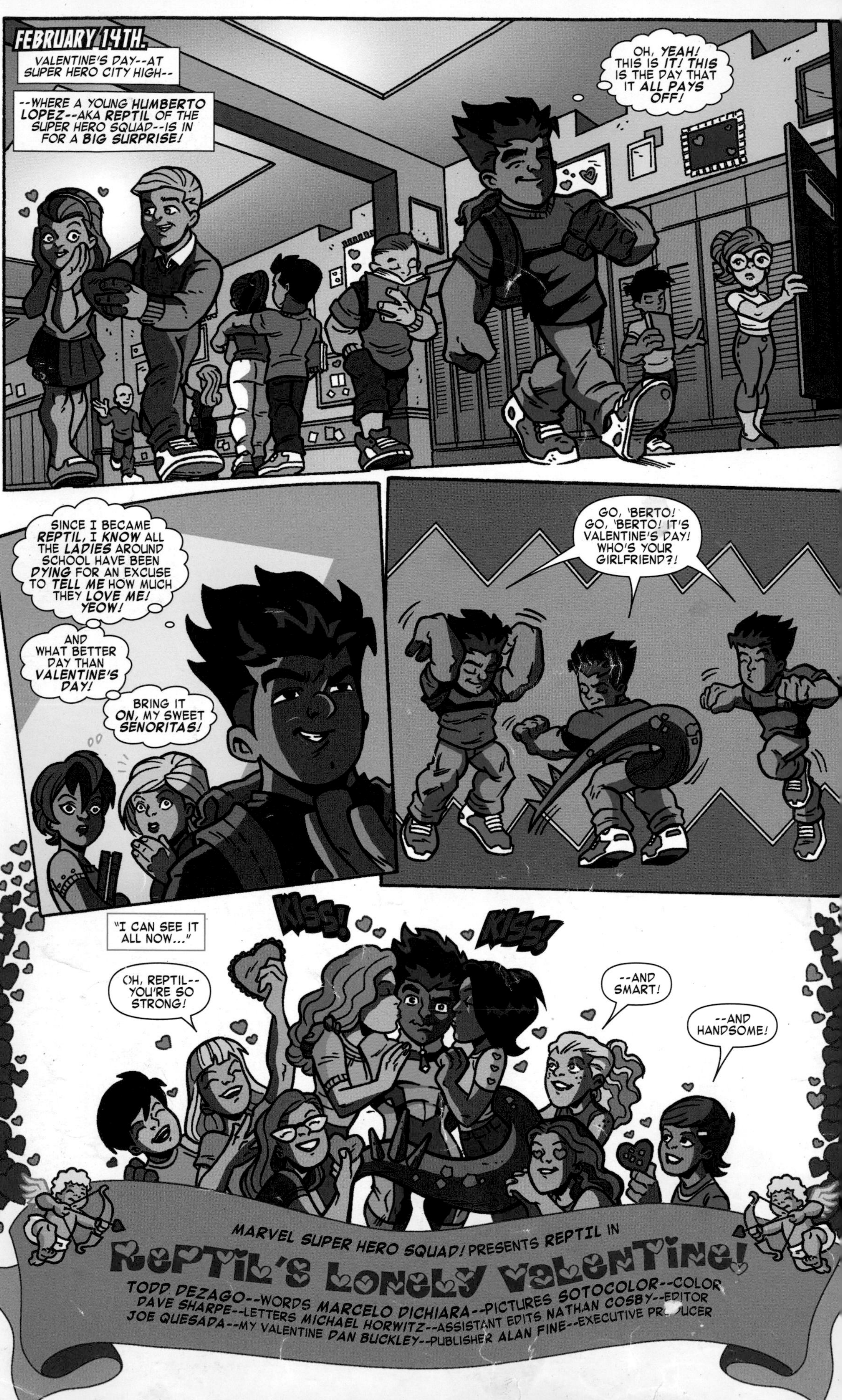
FEBRUARY 14TH.
VALENTINE'S DAY--AT SUPER HERO CITY HIGH--
--WHERE A YOUNG HUMBERTO LOPEZ--AKA REPTIL OF THE SUPER HERO SQUAD--IS IN FOR A BIG SURPRISE!
OH, YEAH! THIS IS IT! THIS IS THE DAY THAT IT ALL PAYS OFF!
SINCE I BECAME REPTIL, I KNOW ALL THE LADIES AROUND SCHOOL HAVE BEEN DYING FOR AN EXCUSE TO TELL ME HOW MUCH THEY LOVE ME! YEOW!
AND WHAT BETTER DAY THAN VALENTINE'S DAY!
BRING IT ON, MY SWEET SENORITAS!
GO, 'BERTO! GO, 'BERTO! IT'S VALENTINE'S DAY! WHO'S YOUR GIRLFRIEND?!
"I CAN SEE IT ALL NOW..."
KISS!
KISS!
OH, REPTIL-- YOU'RE SO STRONG!
--AND SMART!
--AND HANDSOME!
MARVEL SUPER HERO SQUAD! PRESENTS REPTIL IN
REPTIL'S LONELY VALENTINE!
TODD DEZAGO--WORDS MARCELO DICHIARA--PICTURES SOTOCOLOR--COLOR
DAVE SHARPE--LETTERS MICHAEL HORWITZ--ASSISTANT EDITS NATHAN COSBY--EDITOR
JOE QUESADA--MY VALENTINE DAN BUCKLEY--PUBLISHER ALAN FINE--EXECUTIVE PRODUCER

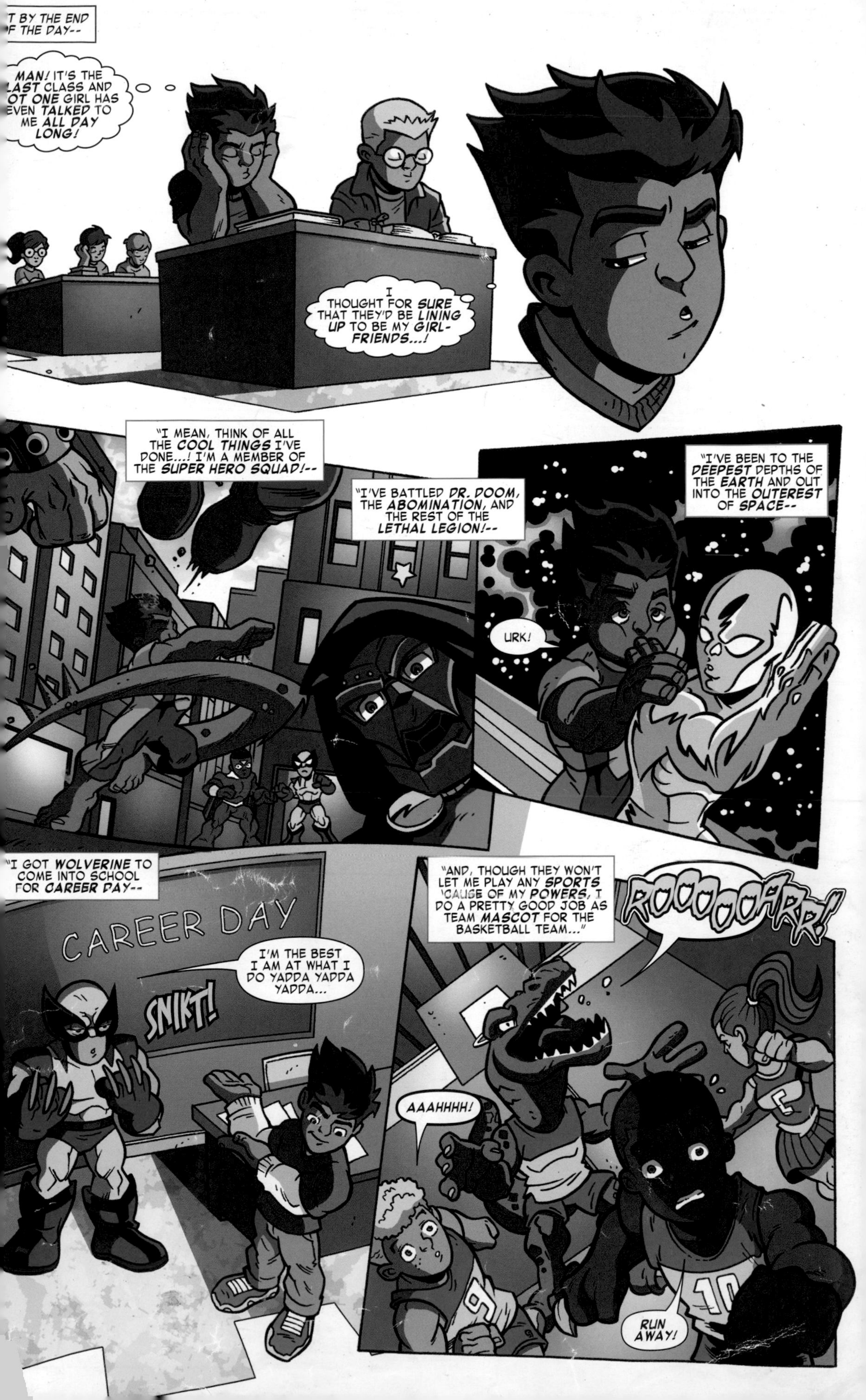

T BY THE END
F THE DAY--
MAN! IT'S THE LAST CLASS AND OT ONE GIRL HAS EVEN TALKED TO ME ALL DAY LONG!
I THOUGHT FOR SURE THAT THEY'D BE LINING UP TO BE MY GIRL-FRIENDS...!
"I MEAN, THINK OF ALL THE COOL THINGS I'VE DONE...! I'M A MEMBER OF THE SUPER HERO SQUAD!--
"I'VE BATTLED DR. DOOM, THE ABOMINATION, AND THE REST OF THE LETHAL LEGION!--
"I'VE BEEN TO THE DEEPEST DEPTHS OF THE EARTH AND OUT INTO THE OUTEREST OF SPACE--
URK!
"I GOT WOLVERINE TO COME INTO SCHOOL FOR CAREER DAY--
CAREER DAY
I'M THE BEST I AM AT WHAT I DO YADDA YADDA YADDA...
SNIKT!
"AND, THOUGH THEY WON'T LET ME PLAY ANY SPORTS 'CAUSE OF MY POWERS, I DO A PRETTY GOOD JOB AS TEAM MASCOT FOR THE BASKETBALL TEAM..."
ROOOOOARR!
AAAHHHH!
RUN AWAY!

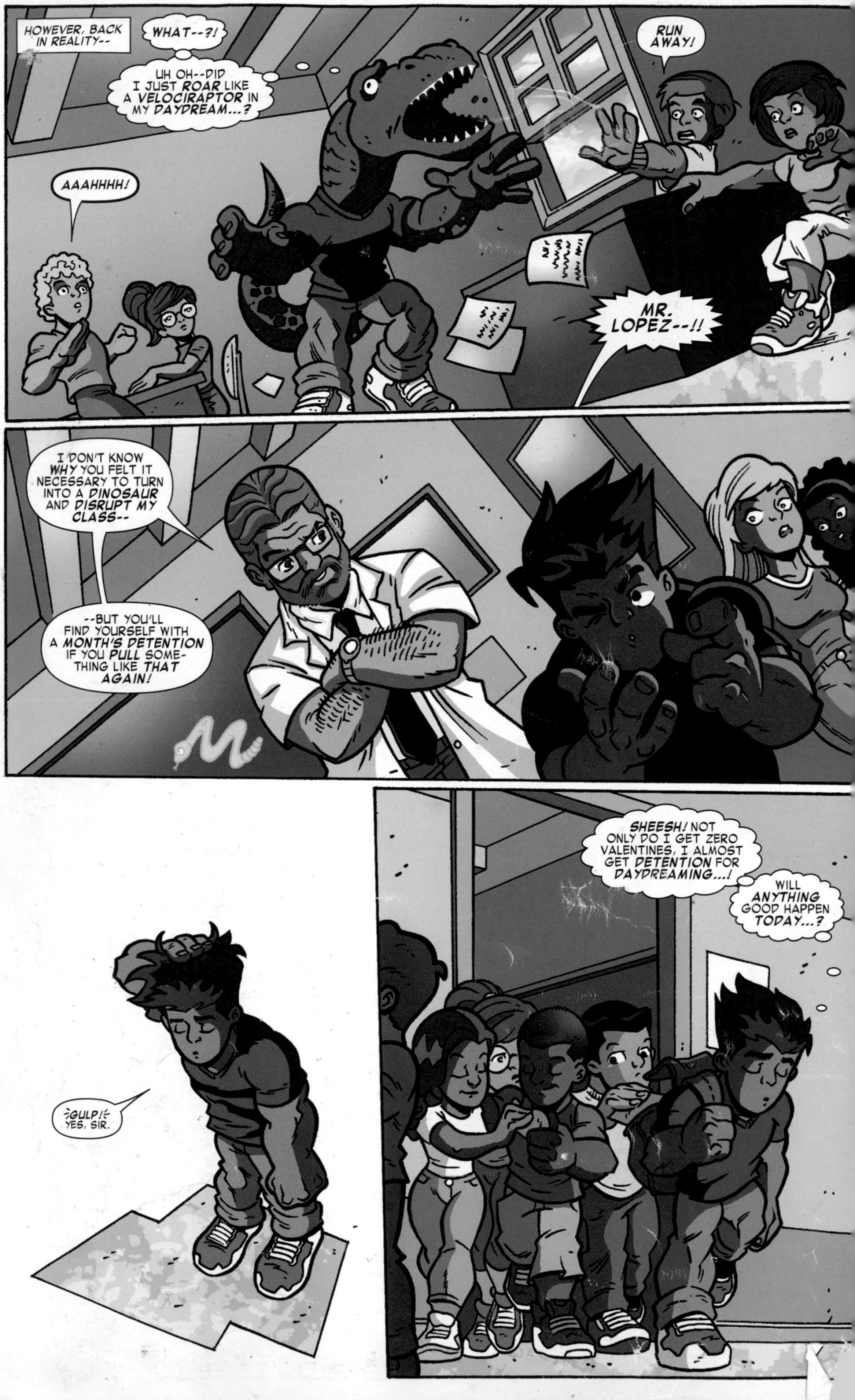
HOWEVER, BACK IN REALITY--
WHAT--?!
UH OH--DID I JUST ROAR LIKE A VELOCIRAPTOR IN MY DAYDREAM...?
RUN AWAY!
AAAHHHH!
MR. LOPEZ--!!
I DON'T KNOW WHY YOU FELT IT NECESSARY TO TURN INTO A DINOSAUR AND DISRUPT MY CLASS--
--BUT YOU'LL FIND YOURSELF WITH A MONTH'S DETENTION IF YOU PULL SOME-THING LIKE THAT AGAIN!
GULP! YES, SIR.
SHEESH! NOT ONLY DO I GET ZERO VALENTINES, I ALMOST GET DETENTION FOR DAYDREAMING...!
WILL ANYTHING GOOD HAPPEN TODAY...?

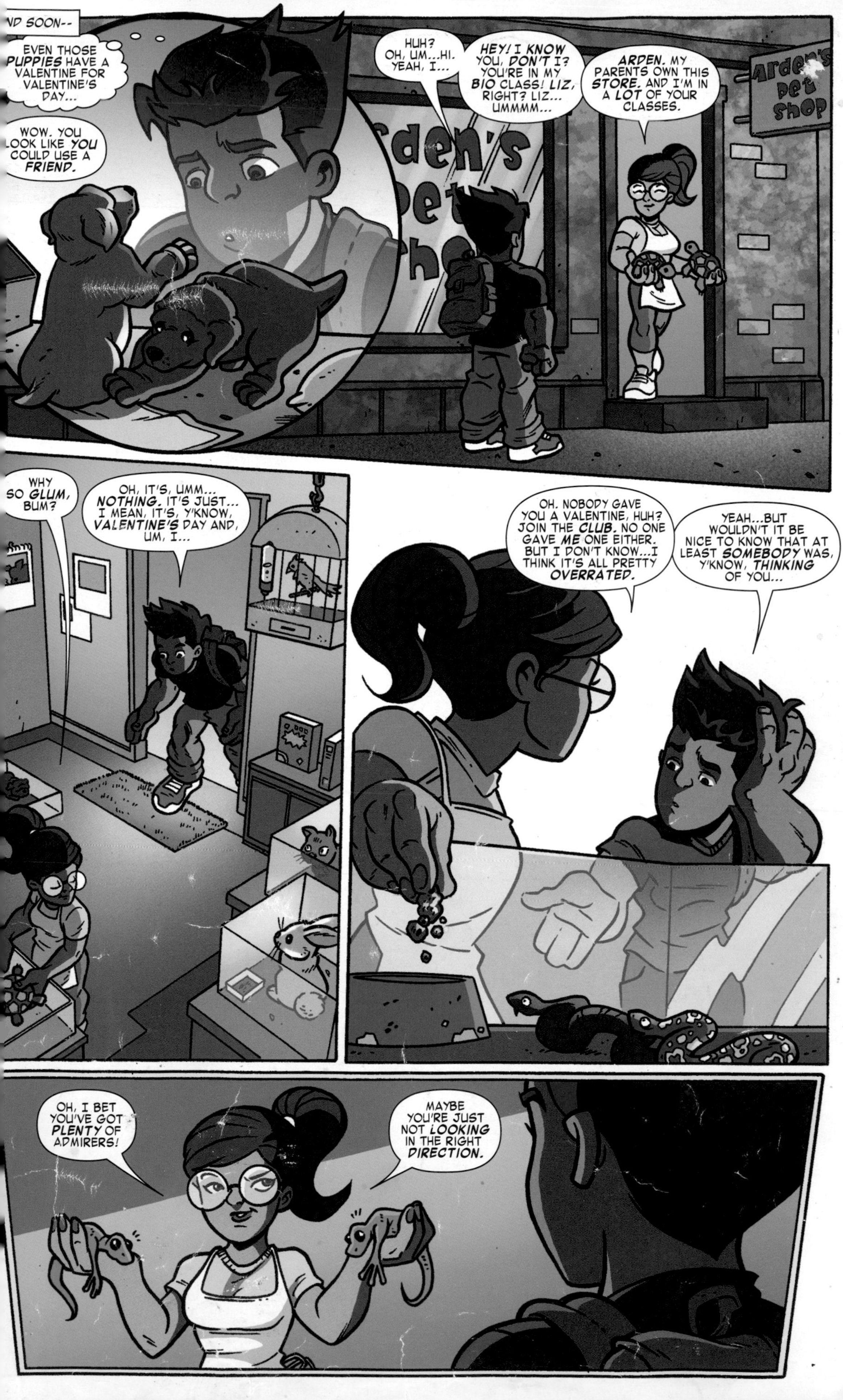
ND SOON--
EVEN THOSE PUPPIES HAVE A VALENTINE FOR VALENTINE'S DAY...
WOW. YOU LOOK LIKE YOU COULD USE A FRIEND.
HUH? OH, UM...HI. YEAH, I...
HEY! I KNOW YOU, DON'T I? YOU'RE IN MY BIO CLASS! LIZ, RIGHT? LIZ... UMMMM...
ARDEN. MY PARENTS OWN THIS STORE. AND I'M IN A LOT OF YOUR CLASSES.
Arden's Pet Shop
WHY SO GLUM, BUM?
OH, IT'S, UMM... NOTHING. IT'S JUST... I MEAN, IT'S, Y'KNOW, VALENTINE'S DAY AND, UM, I...
OH. NOBODY GAVE YOU A VALENTINE, HUH? JOIN THE CLUB. NO ONE GAVE ME ONE EITHER. BUT I DON'T KNOW...I THINK IT'S ALL PRETTY OVERRATED.
YEAH...BUT WOULDN'T IT BE NICE TO KNOW THAT AT LEAST SOMEBODY WAS, Y'KNOW, THINKING OF YOU...
OH, I BET YOU'VE GOT PLENTY OF ADMIRERS!
MAYBE YOU'RE JUST NOT LOOKING IN THE RIGHT DIRECTION.

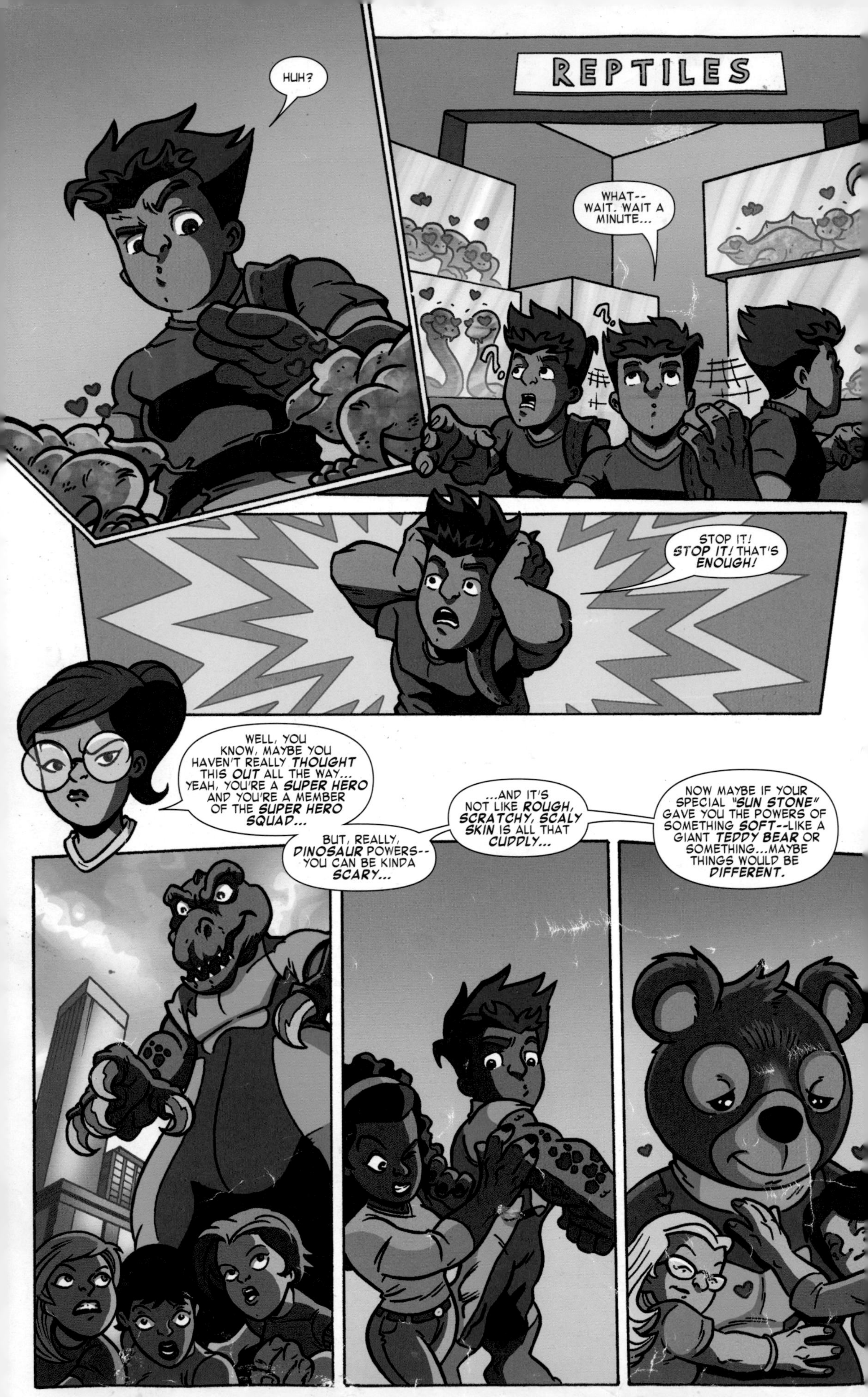
HUH?
REPTILES
WHAT-- WAIT. WAIT A MINUTE...
STOP IT! STOP IT! THAT'S ENOUGH!
WELL, YOU KNOW, MAYBE YOU HAVEN'T REALLY THOUGHT THIS OUT ALL THE WAY... YEAH, YOU'RE A SUPER HERO AND YOU'RE A MEMBER OF THE SUPER HERO SQUAD...
BUT, REALLY, DINOSAUR POWERS-- YOU CAN BE KINDA SCARY...
...AND IT'S NOT LIKE ROUGH, SCRATCHY, SCALY SKIN IS ALL THAT CUDDLY...
NOW MAYBE IF YOUR SPECIAL "SUN STONE" GAVE YOU THE POWERS OF SOMETHING SOFT--LIKE A GIANT TEDDY BEAR OR SOMETHING...MAYBE THINGS WOULD BE DIFFERENT.

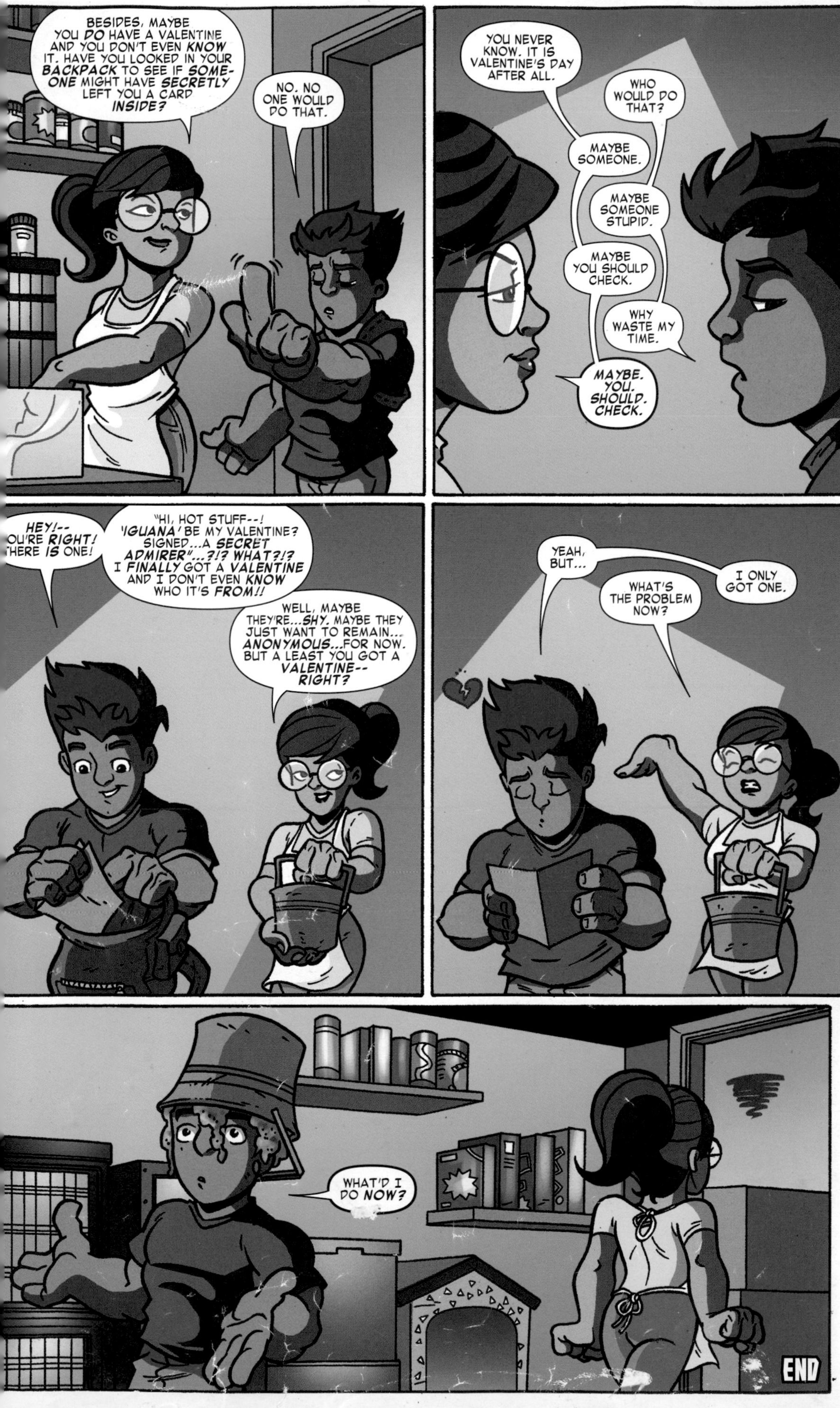
BESIDES, MAYBE YOU DO HAVE A VALENTINE AND YOU DON'T EVEN KNOW IT. HAVE YOU LOOKED IN YOUR BACKPACK TO SEE IF SOME-ONE MIGHT HAVE SECRETLY LEFT YOU A CARD INSIDE?
NO. NO ONE WOULD DO THAT.
YOU NEVER KNOW. IT IS VALENTINE'S DAY AFTER ALL.
WHO WOULD DO THAT?
MAYBE SOMEONE.
MAYBE SOMEONE STUPID.
MAYBE YOU SHOULD CHECK.
WHY WASTE MY TIME.
MAYBE. YOU. SHOULD. CHECK.
HEY!-- OU'RE RIGHT! THERE IS ONE!
"HI, HOT STUFF--! 'IGUANA' BE MY VALENTINE? SIGNED...A SECRET ADMIRER"...?!? WHAT?!? I FINALLY GOT A VALENTINE AND I DON'T EVEN KNOW WHO IT'S FROM!!
WELL, MAYBE THEY'RE...SHY. MAYBE THEY JUST WANT TO REMAIN... ANONYMOUS...FOR NOW. BUT A LEAST YOU GOT A VALENTINE-- RIGHT?
YEAH, BUT...
I ONLY GOT ONE.
WHAT'S THE PROBLEM NOW?
WHAT'D I DO NOW?
END

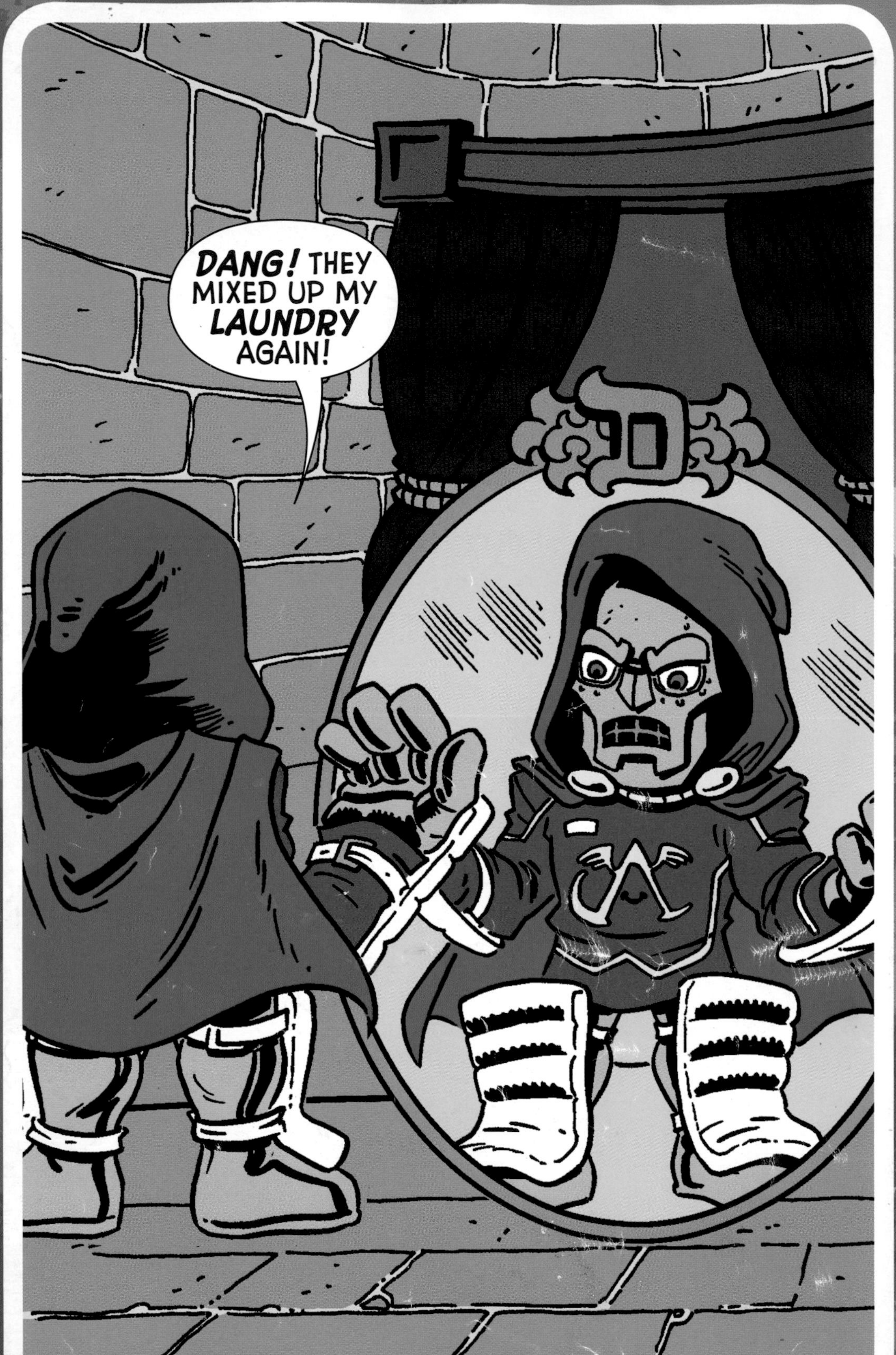
DANG! THEY MIXED UP MY LAUNDRY AGAIN!

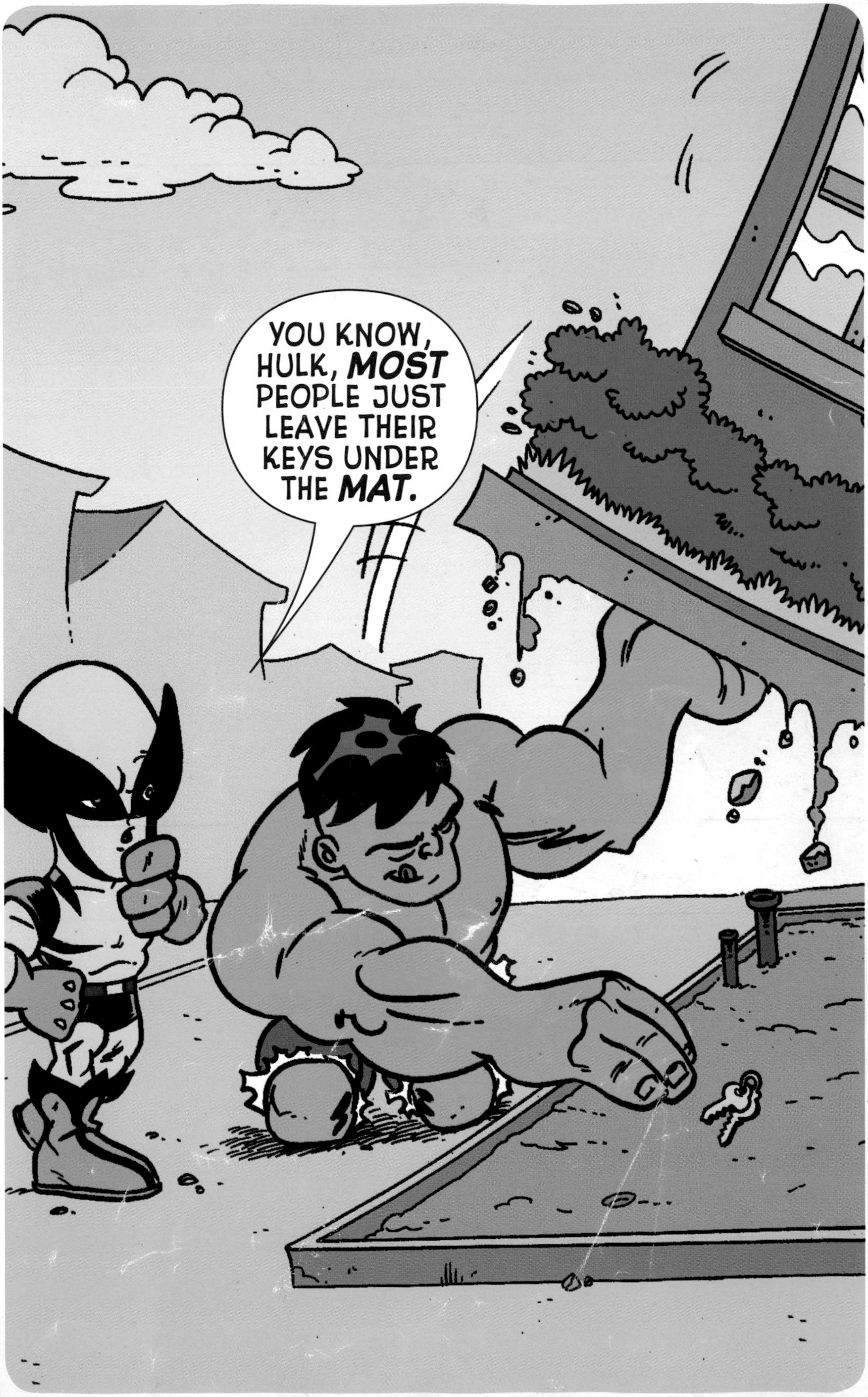
YOU KNOW, HULK, **MOST** PEOPLE JUST LEAVE THEIR KEYS UNDER THE **MAT.**

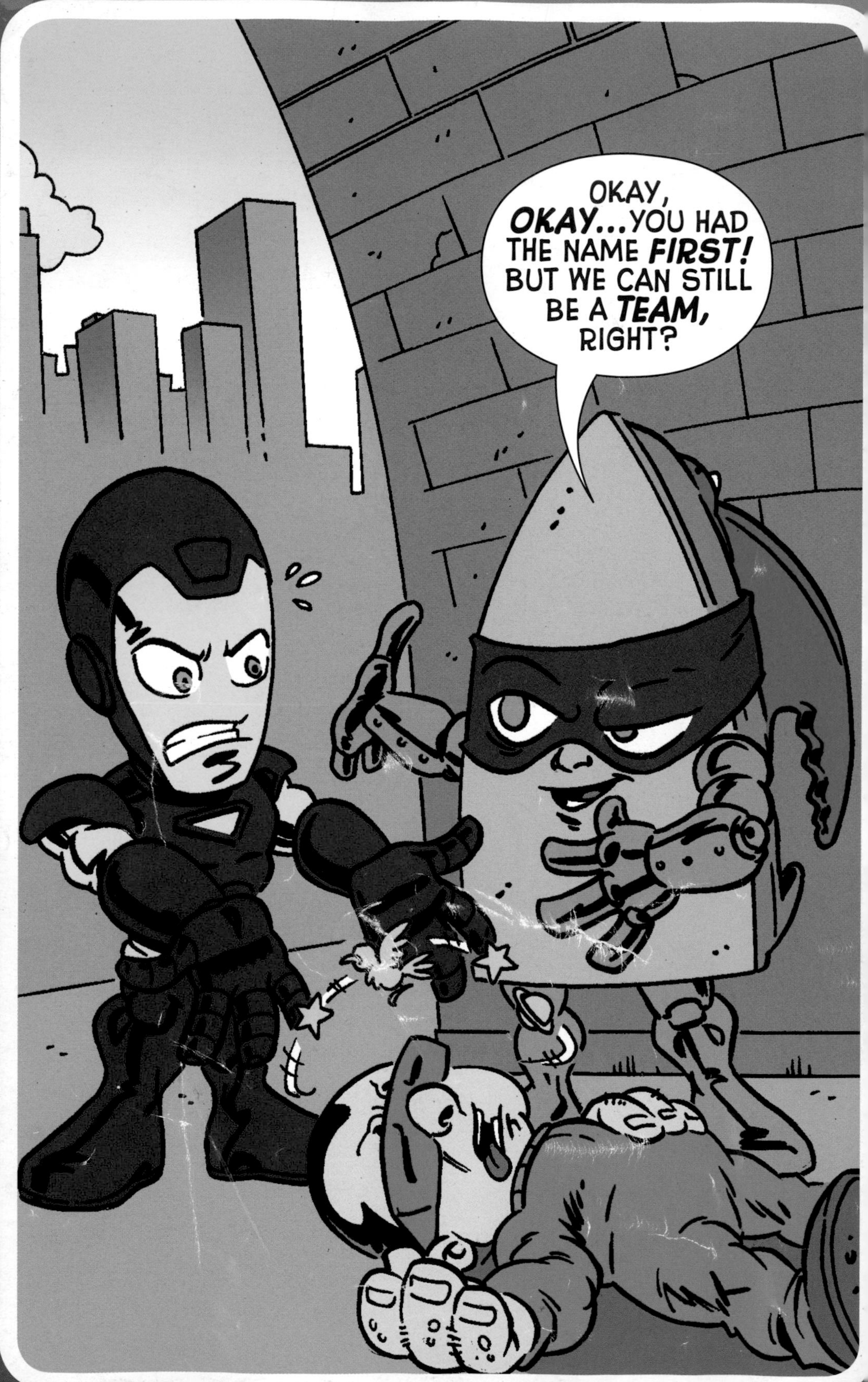
OKAY, OKAY...YOU HAD THE NAME FIRST! BUT WE CAN STILL BE A TEAM, RIGHT?

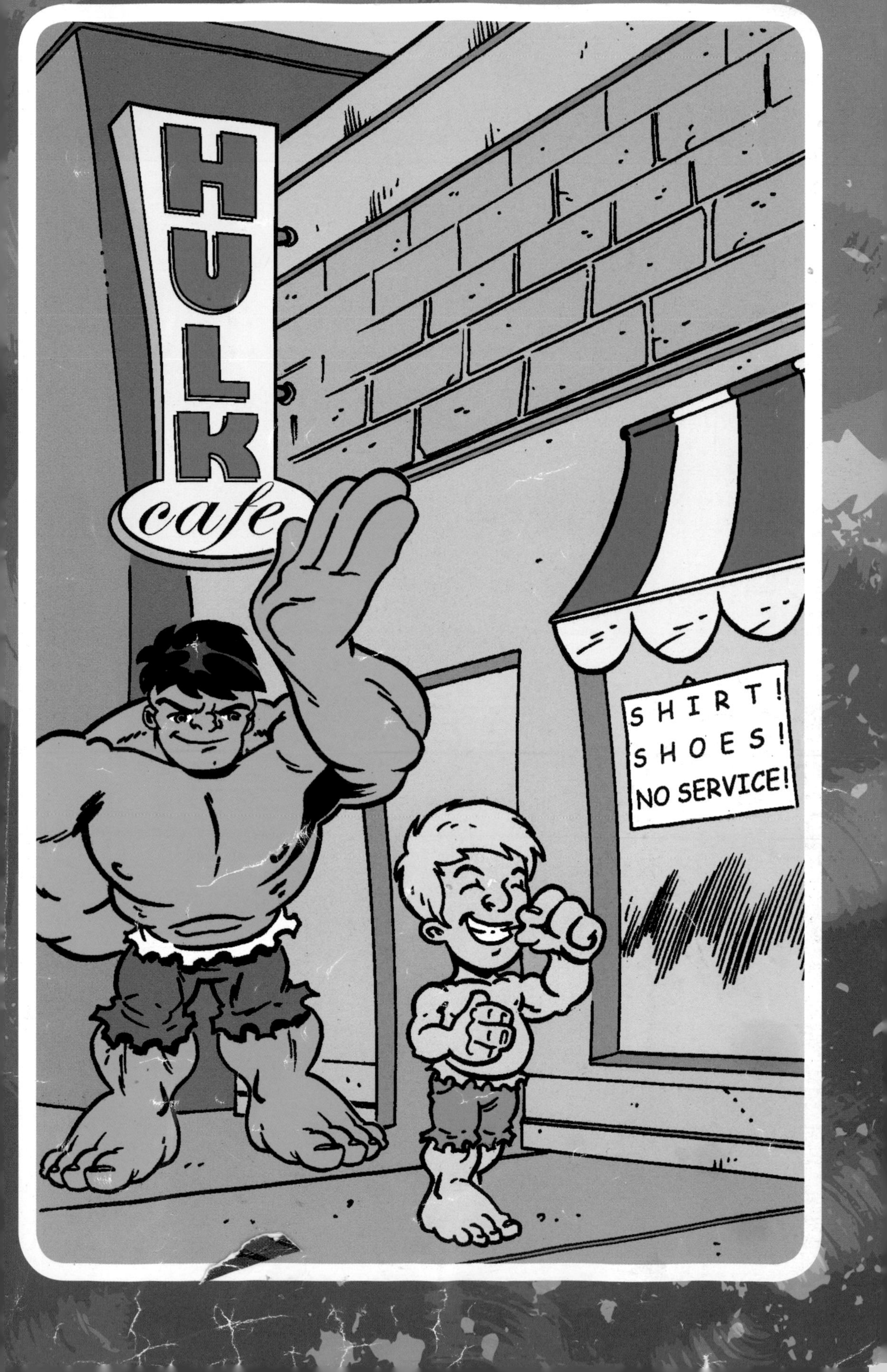
HULK
cafe
SHIRT!
SHOES!
NO SERVICE!

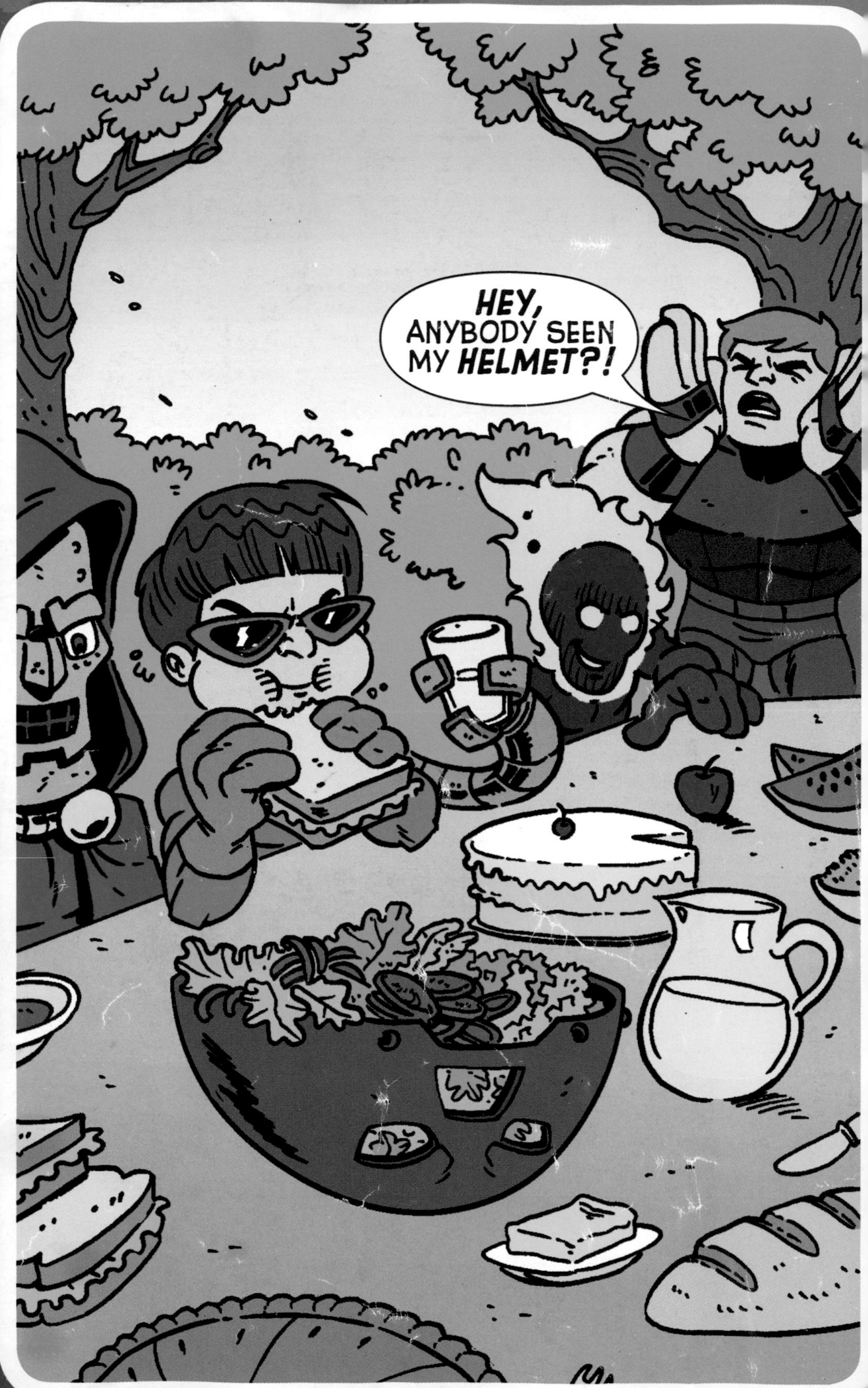
HEY, ANYBODY SEEN MY HELMET?!